YES! CAPRA CHAPBOOK SERIES

1. Henry Miller. ON TURNING EIGHTY.
2. James D. Houston. AN OCCURRENCE AT NORMAN'S BURGER CASTLE.
3. Anais Nin. PARIS REVISITED.
4. Faye Kicknosway. O. YOU CAN WALK ON THE SKY? GOOD.
5. Lawrence Durrell. THE PLANT-MAGIC MAN.
6. Richard de Mille. TWO QUALMS & A QUIRK.
8. Carlos Reyes. THE PRISONER.
9. Andrei Codrescu. A SERIOUS MORNING.
10. Diane di Prima. LOBA: Part 1.
11. Ross Macdonald. ON CRIME WRITING.
12. Barry Gifford. KEROUAC'S TOWN.
13. Ray Bradbury. ZEN & THE ART OF WRITING.
14. Lynn Sukenick. HOUDINI.
15. Jack Hirschman. CANTILLATIONS.
16. William Richardson. THE WOUND.
17. Peter Beagle. LILA THE WEREWOLF.
18. Victor Perera. THE LOCH NESS MONSTER WATCHERS.
19. Clayton Barbeau. DANTE AND GENTUCCA.
20. Colin Wilson. TREE BY TOLKIEN

TREE
BY
TOLKIEN

✣✣✣ BY ✣✣✣

COLIN
WILSON

1974

CAPRA PRESS

SANTA BARBARA

Drawings by Caitlin Mackintosh.

ISBN   0-912264-96-9   (pa.)
ISBN   0-912264-97-7   (cl.)

Capra Press, 631 State Street
Santa Barbara, California 93101

Tree by Tolkien

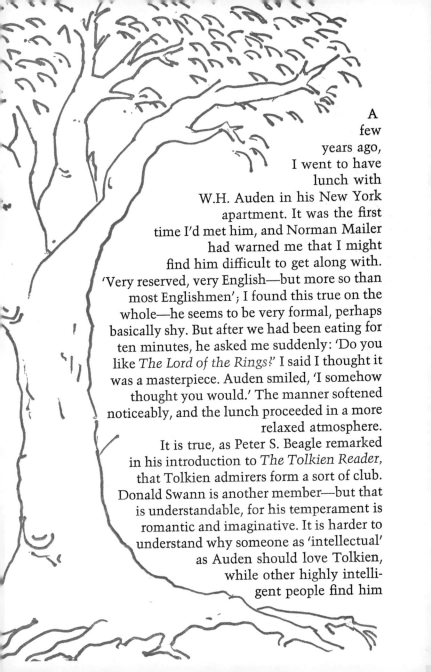

A
few
years ago,
I went to have
lunch with
W.H. Auden in his New York
apartment. It was the first
time I'd met him, and Norman Mailer
had warned me that I might
find him difficult to get along with.
'Very reserved, very English—but more so than
most Englishmen'; I found this true on the
whole—he seems to be very formal, perhaps
basically shy. But after we had been eating for
ten minutes, he asked me suddenly: 'Do you
like *The Lord of the Rings?*' I said I thought it
was a masterpiece. Auden smiled, 'I somehow
thought you would.' The manner softened
noticeably, and the lunch proceeded in a more
relaxed atmosphere.
It is true, as Peter S. Beagle remarked
in his introduction to *The Tolkien Reader*,
that Tolkien admirers form a sort of club.
Donald Swann is another member—but that
is understandable, for his temperament is
romantic and imaginative. It is harder to
understand why someone as 'intellectual'
as Auden should love Tolkien,
while other highly intelligent people find him

somehow revolting. (When I mentioned to a widely read friend—who is also an excellent critic—that I intended to write an essay on Tolkien, he said: 'Good, it's time somebody really exploded that bubble', taking it completely for granted that it would be an attack.) Angus Wilson told me in 1956 that he thought *The Lord of the Rings* was 'don's whimsy' (although he may have changed his mind since then).

I first tried to read the book in about 1954, when only two volumes were out. I already knew a number of people who raved about Tolkien, but who seemed unable to explain precisely why they thought him so significant. I tried the first twenty pages of Volume One, decided this was too much like Enid Blyton, and gave it up for another ten years. In the early sixties, I started to work on a book about imaginative literature, triggered by the discovery of H.P. Lovecraft; John Comley, a psychologist friend (who had himself published a couple of good novels) asked me if I didn't intend to include Tolkien in the book. I said: 'I thought he was pretty dreadful.' 'He's *very* good.' So I bought the three volume edition of *Lord of the Rings*, and started to read it in bed one morning. The absurd result was that I stayed in bed for three days, and read straight through it. What so impressed me on that first reading was the self-containedness of Tolkien's world. I suppose there *are* a few novelists who have created worlds that are uniquely their own—Faulkner, for example, or Dickens. But since

8

their world is fairly close to the actual world, it cannot really be called a unique *creation*. The only parallel that occurs to me is the Wagner Ring cycle, that one can only enter as if taking a holiday on a strange planet.

I have read the book through a couple of times since—once aloud to my children. On re-reading, one notices the sentimentality. I could really do with less of Tom Bombadil, and Gimli's endless talk about the Lady of Lothlorien; but it hardly detracts from the total achievement. But on the second reading, I also noticed how Tolkien achieves the basic effect of the book—by slipping in, rather quietly, passages of 'fine writing'. Not really 'purple passages' in the manner of some of the Victorians (the 'Penny Whistle' chapter of Meredith's *Richard Feverel* is the obvious example). They are too unobtrusive for that.

'Almost at once the sun seemed to sink into the trees behind them. They thought of the slanting light of evening glittering on the Brandywine River, and the windows of Bucklebury beginning to gleam with hundreds of lights. Great shadows fell across them; trunks and branches of trees hung dark and threatening over the path. White mists began to rise and curl on the surface of the river and stray about the roots of the trees upon its borders. Out of the very ground at their feet a shadowy steam arose and mingled with the swiftly falling dusk.'

This is from 'The Old Forest' chapter, and in a sense it is functional. There is nothing here as

embarrassing as in the 'Piper at the Gates of Dawn' chapter of *The Wind in the Willows*. I suppose what comes over most clearly from all this is that Tolkien is *enjoying* creating the scene, revelling in it; it has an air of play, like baby seals chasing one another in a stream of bubbles. This is certainly the basic strength and charm of the book. And it may—this is only a guess—explain why Tolkien is taking so long to produce the huge epic on the dwarves that he promised ten years ago; this kind of spontaneity seldom comes twice.

I find it interesting to recall those comments on Tolkien, made by friends in the early fifties—precisely because they *couldn't* explain why they thought him 'important'. They certainly *felt* him important, something more than a writer of fantasy or fairy tales. It is also significant that there has been so little written about him, in spite of his appeal to 'intellectuals'; I known only the essay by Beagle (already mentioned) and Edmund Wilson's attack in *The Bit Between My Teeth*. This makes it an interesting challenge—to define the exact nature and extent of Tolkien's importance.

One night begin by considering that Wilson essay, for Wilson is a good critic, who leans over backwards to try to understand why anyone should admire *The Lord of the Rings*. What Wilson says, basically, is that the book is 'essentially a children's book—a children's book which has somehow got out of hand, since, instead of directing it at the juvenile market, the author has indulged himself in developing fantasy for its own sake'.

He ends by accounting for the popularity of the book by remarking that many people, especially in Britain, have a lifelong appetite for juvenile trash.

Fortunately, Tolkien's output has not been immense —fortunately for the critic, I mean. So it is not quite as difficult as it might be to trace the development of his characteristic ideas.

Tolkien was born in 1892—an interesting fact in itself. It means that by the time he was ten years old—the age at which children begin to find their own way in literature—he was living in the middle of a literary era of great vitality and complexity. The best-sellers of the day were Kipling, Rider Haggard, Conan Doyle, Maurice Hewlett and Anthony Hope—all romantics, all influenced by Stevenson. But new figures were emerging, equally romantic, but also intellectuals—Wells, Shaw, Chesterton and Belloc. We now tend to be dismissive about this era, thinking of it as a kind of inferior Victorian twilight, bearing the same relation to the real thing that Richard Strauss's music bears to Wagner. This is unfair and inaccurate. We are now living in an age of literary exhaustion; we get used to the bleak landscape. Cyril Connolly said that the writer's business is to produce masterpieces; but what masterpieces have been produced in the past fifty years? *Ulysses, The Waste Land,* Musil's *Man Without Qualities;* a few people would include Kafka, perhaps E.M. Forster, Hermann Broch's *Sleepwalkers,* Mann's *Magic Mountain.* And what more recently? We have to look

back over several decades to find writers of this level of 'significance'. As to contemporaries: Amis, Osborne, Gunter Grass, Philip Roth, Robbe-Grillet . . . no one among these shows any sign of developing the stature of a Shaw or Joyce. We simply take it for granted that nothing much has happened for decades. In 1902, things *had* been happening for decades, and they shonwed no sign of slackening; the age of Dickens and Carlyle gave way to the age of Stevenson, Hardy, Meredith, Kipling. The English were discovering Tolstoy and Dostoevsky, Strindberg, Ibsen, Zola, Nietzsche, Maeterlinck. Things seemed to be happening everywhere; it was a great melting pot, shooting off sparks of literary talent. It was still a romantic era, as lively as the *Sturm und drang* period of a hundred years earlier—except that the romanticism now had a distinctly optimistic flavour. By the time this era came to an end—in 1914—Tolkien was twenty-two, and his formative period was over.

I strongly suspect that Chesterton was the major influence during this period. The clues are scattered throughout the essay *On Fairy-Stories* (delivered at St. Andrews in 1938.) Speaking, for example, about suspension of disbelief, the 'enchanted state' which some people can achieve when watching a cricket match, he says: 'I can achieve (more or less) willing suspension of disbelief, when I am held there and supported by some other motive that will keep away boredom: for instance, a wild, heraldic preference for dark blue rather than light' —a sentence that could easily have been written by

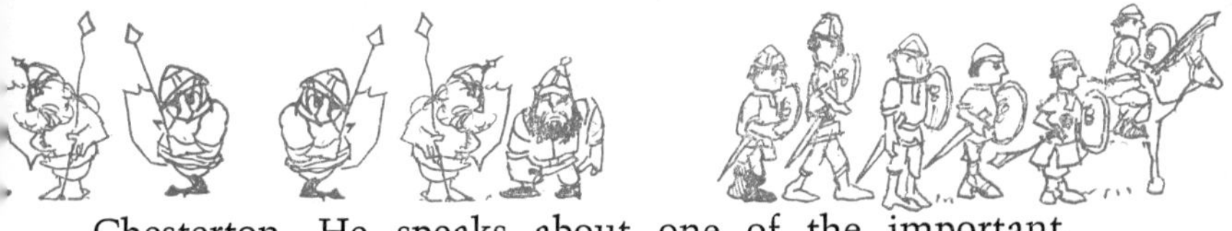

Chesterton. He speaks about one of the important functions of the fairy story, to produce a state of 'recovery', 'regaining of a clear view'. 'We need . . . to clean our windows; so that the things seen clearly may be freed from the drab blur of triteness or familiarity—from possessiveness.' He then goes on to speak of '*Mooreeffoc*' or Chestertonian fantasy. '*Mooreeffoc* is a fantastic word, but it could be seen written up in every town in this land. It is Coffee-room, viewed from inside through a glass door, as it was seen by Dickens on a dark London day; and it was used by Chesterton to denote the queerness of things that have become trite, when they are seen suddenly from a new angle.'

Readers of early Chesterton books—*Napoleon of Notting Hill, The Man Who Was Thursday,* the early Father Brown stories—will recollect that Disneyland atmosphere. 'It was one of those journeys on which a man perpetually feels that now at last he must have come to the end of the universe, and then finds he has only come to the beginning of Tufnell Park, London died away in draggled taverns and dreary scrubs, and then was unaccountably born again in blazing high streets and blatant hotels . . .' *What* Chesterton is describing here (in *The Blue Cross)* might have come out of a novel by Graham Greene; but the way in which he describes it makes it somehow mysterious and exhilarating. 'Abruptly one bulging and gas-lit window broke the blue twilight like a bull's eye lantern; and Valentin stopped an instant before a little garish sweetstuff shop.' Dickens occasion-

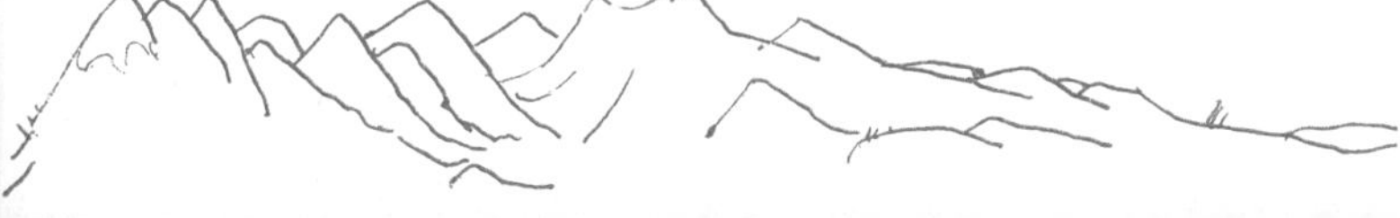

ally commanded that magic; for example, in *Pickwick Papers* and *A Christmas Carol*; and J.B. Priestley catches it in a few of his novels. Tolkien set out to take it out of 'this world', to create it in isolation, or rather, in its own setting, in 'fairy land'.

This immediately suggests another name—W.B. Yeats. Not only because Yeats wrote about fairies, but because he attached a particular symbolic meaning to them. There is a sharp dichotomy in Yeats between 'this world' and a world of deeper *meaning* that poets glimpse in moments of intensity. There is no space here to discuss this point at length; besides, I have done so elsewhere.* But I would suggest that the dichotomy between 'this world' and that more meaningful reality is a false one; what is at issue is an *attitude*, like the difference between Greene and Chesterton. Tolkien grasps this when he says, echoing Blake: 'We need . . . to clean our windows.' In certain exhilarated moods, the poet sees the world as endlessly exciting and interesting; in such states of insight, it seems clear to him that all one needs is intelligence and imagination, and the vision can be renewed every day. The really baffling thing is why this vision is so difficult to sustain. The straightforward view is that most human beings are tied down to dreary everyday affairs, like Dickens in his blacking factory or Wells in his drapery emporium, and that all the embryonic Dickenses and Wellses need is freedom. We soon discover that the problem is more complicated than

*In a long essay in *Poetry and Mysticism* (1970).

14

that; even intelligent and imaginative men are often bored. For some reason, this sense of the world as an endlessly meaningful place slips away from us when we need it most. Boredom is one of the great mysteries of psychology. It seems to be a matter of *focussing*, like focussing a very powerful microscope or telescope; and we are just not very good at focussing. 'Focussing' occurs in moods of serenity or of creative excitement. Its greatest enemy is the ordinary, noisy distractions of everyday reality. So in his early poetry, Yeats continually attacks this reality—'The wrong of unshapely things is a wrong too great to be told' (echoing the forger Wainewright, who murdered his sister-in-law because he said he couldn't stand her thick ankles)— and creates a world of misty trees and autumn leaves and men who wander off into the land of the Faery. And seventy or so years after Yeats wrote 'The Song of Wandering Aengus', Tolkien produced *Smith of Wootton Major*, a fable that might have been published in the Yellow Book with Aubrey Beardsley drawings. Wootton Major is one of those rustic villages in an unnamed country that might be next door to Hobbit-land, and the Great Cook of the village produces a magnificent cake every twenty-four years. But when the story opens, the present cook has been wandering off for mysterious absences (from which he returns merrier than usual), and he finally goes away permanently, leaving behind a strange apprentice whom he has brought back from his wanderings. Next time the Great

Cake is baked, the apprentice slips into it a silver star—a fairy gift—and one of the children swallows it. This child—the [black]smith of the title—grows up to become a wanderer between the village and the land of Faery. Various adventures are described—with a brevity and arbitrariness uncharacteristic of Tolkien—and at the end of the story, the smith hands back the star, his passport to Faery land, and it is passed on to another child through the Great Cake. The apprentice turns out to be the King of the Faery in disguise. All this is fairly clear. The Cooks who make the Great Cake are somehow the intermediaries between the Faery and 'the world' (it is Tolkien who makes the distinction); perhaps they are story tellers. The children who swallow the star are the poets—like Yeats or Tolkien—who become wanderers between two worlds. Apart from an earlier fable, *Leaf by Niggle,* this is the most 'symbolic' of Tolkien's stories, scarcely a children's story at all. The content is hardly profound; in some ways, it could be called naive; it might have been a story by Walter de la Mare, with its simple message of turning away from the everyday world. In fact, only one step away from *Peter Pan.* Yet naive or not, the problem Tolkien is writing about is fundamental, and its importance and relevance have not diminished since the time of Yeats and Barrie. This is a point that Edmund Wilson completely failed to grasp in his essay.

There are a few more 'influences' to be noted. The period of Chesterton's early books was also the period

of Belloc's *Path to Rome* (1902), the kind of travel book that can be enjoyed even by people who hate travel books. Belloc describes how he finished his military service at Toul, in Alsace, and decided to walk across Switzerland to Rome. There are sketches—by Belloc himself—of great misty views, and the front cover of the first edition (which I bought years ago for two shillings) has a coloured inset of a blue sky with white clouds and a road that goes through a forest on a mountainside. It is 'escape' literature in the best sense, and Belloc never again captured that same invigorating sense of freedom and great open vistas, although he tried hard in *Four Men* and *The Cruise of the Nona*. I have no idea whether Tolkien ever read *The Path to Rome* (for although I wrote to him and asked him various questions at the time I wrote *The Strength to Dream*—and he answered patiently and kindly—I forgot to ask about 'influences'), but it seems to me that this book above all others could have triggered his lifelong obsession with journeys and heroes who set out to walk towards the mountains.

So, I think, could the work of another writer whose work is never mentioned by respectable critics: Jeffrey Farnol. His first book, *The Broad Highway*, came out in 1910, and brought him overnight fame, running into endless impressions. Farnol used the same plot again and again, always with a certain success, for it possesses a potent charm—the young man setting out on the open road with a few shillings in his pocket, in search of

romance, adventure and fortune. The 'adventures'—
with highwaymen, Bow Street runners, wicked squires
(who have kidnapped fair ladies), bad-tempered pugi-
lists, Regency bucks—may be absurd, and, after the first
few books, repetitive, but the real power of the story
springs from the poetry of freedom: the hero striding
cheerfully along dark lanes in the starlight, watching
the sky turn pale and hearing the first birds, then stop-
ping to wash in a brook before he approaches the country inn with the smell of frying bacon floating through
the windows. . . . Anyone who read Farnol in his teens
will never forget him. He must have tempted many
children to run away from home. Tolkien was eighteen
when *The Broad Highway* appeared; I find it inconceiv-
able that he did not read the book and find it absorbing.

Another influence—of Anglo-Saxon and mediaeval
poetry—is altogether more obvious, and, in my view,
less important. Tolkien began as a philologist; his first
publication was *A Middle English Vocabulary* in 1922,
and his second, an edition of the mediaeval romance
Sir Gawain and the Green Knight, (with E.V. Gordon,
1925). There was also an essay on *Chaucer as Philologist* (1934), an essay on *Beowulf: the Monsters and the
Critics* (1937) and an imitation Anglo-Saxon poem *The
Homecoming of Beorhtnoth, Beorhthelm's Son*, (1953).
Edmund Wilson quotes a statement prepared for his
publishers in which Tolkien refers to *The Lord of the
Rings* as a philological game. 'The "stories" were made
rather to provide a world for the languages than the

reverse.' This, it seems to me, is a red-herring, like James's description of *The Turn of the Screw* as 'a fairy tale, pure and simple'. Tolkien may well have derived enormous pleasure from giving the book another dimension of realism with the invention of Elvish and other 'languages', but this modest statement of its aims is plainly an attempt to disarm hostile critics—as it partly disarmed Wilson.

The influence of Anglo-Saxon and mediaeval poetry on Tolkien is quite clear. To begin with, there is his strong tendency to a backward-looking nostalgia, derived in part from Chesterton and Belloc, and their 'two acres and a cow' Distributism. (One should remember that one of Chesterton's best books is on Chaucer.) Next there is the pleasure in the sensual quality of life in the Middle Ages, as portrayed in its poems—great sides of beef cooking over open fires, magnificent feasts, colourful festivities, and so on. (Mervyn Peake is also fascinated by this world in his *Titus Groan* trilogy.) Finally, there is the element of savagery and wildness: the great battles, the burning of Njal, the bleak open moorlands and the lakes that hold monsters like Grendel (perhaps the creepiest monster in literature outside Frankenstein). It is very much an idealised, Chestertonian mediaevalism, rather like that of T.H. White. From *The Lord of the Rings*, one would gather that Tolkien's interest in the Middle Ages is literary and idealistic, not precise and detailed, like that of G.G. Coulton and Huizinga. And it could be argued that the battle scenes

of *The Lord of the Rings* spoil the total effect, that they seem to be part of a completely different book. They certainly interrupt the swift flow of the story. When I first read *The Lord of the Rings* I skipped the whole of the fifth book in order to find out what happens after Frodo is captured by the Orcs, and when I later read it aloud to my children, they again insisted on skipping it. On this occasion, I returned to the fifth book after I had got Frodo and Sam on their road to Mount Doom, but the children seemed to lose interest until we got back to Frodo and Sam.

Finally—in considering 'influences'—one should point out the relationship between Tolkien and T.S. Eliot. *The Waste Land* is an attack on the modern world, and Eliot turns to the past for his symbols of a superior order of reality—the Fisher King, the Rhine maidens, the Grail legend, 'inexplicable splendour of Ionian white and gold'.

'What does the world say, does the whole world stray in high-powered cars on a by-pass way?. . .'

In the essay on fairy tales, Tolkien has some strong words defending the fairy story against charges of 'escapism'. He mentioned that he recently heard 'a clerk of Oxenford' declare that he welcomed 'the prox- imity of mass-production robot factories, and the roar of self-obstructive mechanical traffic because it brought his university into "contact with real life". . .' This view obviously makes Tolkien see red. 'He may have meant that the way men were living and working in the twen-

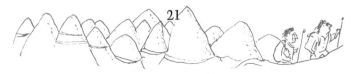

tieth century was increasing in barbarity at an alarming rate, and that the loud demonstration of this in the streets of Oxford might serve as a warning that it is not possible to preserve for long an oasis of sanity in a desert of unreason by mere fences, without actual offensive action (practical and intellectual). I fear he did not. In any case the expression "real life" in this context seems to fall short of academic standards. The notion that motor cars are more "alive" than, say, centaurs or dragons is curious; that they are more "real" than, say, horses is pathetically absurd.' One sentence has a positively Chestertonian ring: 'Fairy stories may invent monsters that fly the air or dwell in the deep, but at least they do not try to escape from heaven or the sea'. He argues that talk about 'escapism' is a misuse of language: why shouldn't a man in gaol try to escape? What he is arguing here—although he does not put it in so many words—is that there is escape *from* reality and escape *to* reality, and that what interests him is the escape *to* reality. It is Yeats's argument with the 'socially conscious' writers of the thirties all over again (expressed most typically, perhaps, in *Lapis Lazuli*). Tolkien argues at some length about street lamps and their ugliness, speaking of his 'disgust for so typical a product of the robot age', and on the next page uses one of his favourite images of life, a tree: 'How real, how startlingly alive is a factory chimney compared with an elm tree; poor obsolete thing, insubstantial dream of an escapist.' It is amusing to remember the use Chesterton

made of the lamp versus tree image in *The Man Who Was Thursday*, when the anarchist declares that the lamp is a symbol of order, ugly and barren when compared with the tree, 'anarchy, splendid in green and gold.' Gabriel Syme, Chesterton's mouthpiece, replies: 'All the same, just at present you only see the tree by the light of the lamp. I wonder when you would ever see the lamp by the light of the tree.'

In the same volume as the essay on fairy stories *(Tree and Leaf)* Tolkien includes a short fable, 'Leaf by Niggle', written shortly after publication of *The Hobbit* (1937). This is an odd little work, almost Kafka-esque. It begins typically 'There was once a little man called Niggle, who had a long journey to make'. But this is not another story of man's search for fairy land. Niggle is a painter who is engaged on a picture that sounds like an illustration for *Lord of the Rings*—mountains, forests, lakes, with an enormous tree in the foreground, a kind of Tree of Life. Niggle is often interrupted by a tiresome neighbour, Parish, a lame man with a sick wife. Parish's only interest is in digging his garden, and he finds Niggle's neglect of his own garden annoying. When he calls on Niggle, he does not even glance at the picture of the tree and fairy landscape. So far, the symbolism is clear enough: Niggle, the visionary artist, but nevertheless a modest little man, working away quietly, minding his own business, trying to capture his vision of fairy land, the 'world of meaning', and Parish, the man-in-the-street, interested only in 'practical' things and always obstructing the artist.

Parish interrupts Niggle as he is trying to finish the picture, and asks him to go and get a doctor for his sick wife. Niggle goes, gets caught in a storm, and catches a cold that confines him to his bed for weeks, destroying his chance of finishing the picture before he sets out on his journey. While he is in bed, a strange Kafka-esque official calls on him and tells him that his neighbour's house is not satisfactory—the implication being that it is Niggle's duty to take care of his neighbour. Niggle's picture would be just the right size to mend a hole in Parish's roof. When Niggle protests 'It's my Picture', the Inspector replies 'I dare say it is. But houses come first. That is the law'. The bewildered artist is ordered to start on his journey, and he sets out quite unprepared. The journey is pure Kafka; he is pushed on to a train, gets out at a station where the porter yells 'Niggle', collapses, and is taken to a workhouse infirmary. This turns out to be a kind of prison where he is made to do boring manual tasks (it sounds like a Soviet labour camp) and spends hours locked in his room in the dark. Then some mysterious 'judges' talk about him so he can overhear them. 'His heart was in the right place.' 'Yes, but it did not function properly. And his head was not screwed on tight enough: he hardly ever thought at all . . . He never got ready for his journey. He was moderately well off, and yet he arrived here almost destitute. . . .' Niggle, it seems, is at fault; but the judges finally agree that he is a good sort and deserves a second chance. 'He took a great deal of pain with leaves.' So Niggle is let out, and sent on another train

journey. This time he finds himself in a kind of Happy Land where his tree is an actuality, and behind it is the visionary country of his picture. His old neighbour Parish—who has also been confined in the workhouse for negligence—joins him, and they now work together to build a cottage with a garden. When this is finished —by this time Niggle has become the practical man and Parish something of a dreamer and slacker—Niggle finally goes off towards his goal in the mountains, leaving Parish to live in the cottage with his wife.

Back in Niggle's old house, only a corner of his canvas remains, a single leaf, and this is put into the museum (hence the title of the story). The place that has been created by Niggle and Parish in cooperation becomes known as 'Niggle's Parish'.

It is an odd little story, most disappointing to children. The 'journey' is quite plainly death—in fact, Tolkien makes something say so at the end of the story, where a councilor remarks that Niggle was worthless to society, and ought to have been sent on his journey much earlier, and consigned to the great Rubbish Heap. Like Yeats, Tolkien is continuing his argument with the socially conscious writers of the thirties. But what precisely is he saying? Niggle is an artist and something of a visionary, but all in a rather bumbling, incompetent manner. This incompetence seems to be the root of his trouble. If he were more ruthless, he would tell Parish to go to hell, and finish his picture. But this, Tolkien implies, is the wrong solution. The Niggle-

Parish conflict is not really necessary; they *can* collaborate fruitfully, and when they do, it becomes clear that Niggle is Parish's superior.

The final judgement, then, is unexpectedly complex. In the conflict between the artist and society, Tolkien comes down on the artist's side—as is to be expected—but he also blames the artist, implying that if he were less vague and incompetent, he could become something more like a leader of society—without, however, compromising his own basic vision. He does not have to become a servant of the State and paint pictures of tractors. . . . But what precisely he *is* supposed to do is left to the imagination.

(I may point out, in parenthesis, that Tolkien's view agrees, unexpectedly, with Bernard Shaw's—as outlined, for example, in *Major Barbara,* where Shaw declares that the artist must come out of his ivory tower and try to become a dominant figure in the society. The question is of particular concern to me; it was at the core of my first book *The Outsider* (1956)—the problem of the relation between the artist and society. The romantics of the 19th century thought that the artist is at war with society, and must be destroyed by it eventually; this is the theme of all Hoffmann's stories. I suggested —in *The Outsider* and the subsequent five books of the 'cycle'— that the fault lies partly with the artist, for preferring pessimism and self-pity to serious thought, and that the 'outsider' must eventually learn to accept his position as a spiritual leader of society. The church once

provided the link between 'outsiders' and society, standing for the world of values, of 'meanings' beyond the present. The artists of the 19th century found themselves without this visible symbol of non-material values, and were, as Hoffmann says, frequently destroyed by society, or by their own destiny of standing outside it. I concluded that they must learn to stand alone, to be twice as strong, for half the problems of our civilisation are due to 'the treason of the intellectual', their tendency to opt out and collapse in self-pity.)

This brings us back to the assertion in the essay on fairy stories, that it is not possible to preserve an oasis of sanity in a desert of unreason 'without actual offensive action (practical and intellectual)'. That is fine; but what offensive action? As far as I can see, Tolkien nowhere suggests an answer to this problem. His own 'defensive action' was justifiable enough if we accept Connolly's view that the artist's business is to produce a masterpiece. For all its sentimentality and its flaws, *The Lord of the Rings* is a masterpiece. Whether it has any practical significance for the present discussion of the artist and society is a different matter.

It seems to me that if we reject Edmund Wilson's view that Tolkien's work is an overgrown children's story of no significance, and accept that it is a part of the great European romantic tradition, attacking the same problems as the tales of Hoffmann, Goethe's *Faust*, De L'Isle Adam's *Axel*, Hesse's *Steppenwolf*, Eliot's *Waste Land*, then we must admit that Tolkien has

weakened his own case by sticking too close to fairy tale traditions. I believe that *The Lord of the Rings* is a significant work of twentieth century literature, as significant as *Remembrance of Things Past* or *The Waste Land*. Its extraordinarily wide appeal—on American campuses, for example—is not due to purely 'escapist' elements. It strikes a chord, as *The Waste Land* did in the twenties, because its symbols constitute a kind of *exploration* of the real world. We still live under a threat of a great oppressive evil; in the west, we identify it with communism; in Russia and China, they identify it with capitalist imperialism; the hydrogen bomb serves as a symbol for both sides. But all imaginative people feel that there are solutions that no politician is far-sighted enough to grasp. Our hope for the future lies in the capacity of the human imagination to reach beyond the present, in our capacity to glimpse vistas of meaning that stretch out endlessly around us. Tolkien's work performs the important function of stimulating this wild, Chestertonian hope for the future. For all I know, Tolkien may think of himself as a pessimist, in the strictly historical sense; i.e. he may see no practical hope for our civilisation. Many intelligent men of his generation feel the same; T.S. Eliot did; the historian A.L. Rowse does; and Arnold Toynbee once told me that he was glad that he was near the end of his life instead of the beginning, because the next few decades were going to be hell for everybody. But in the fairy tale essay, Tolkien states that one of the most im-

portant functions of the fairy tale is to aid 'recovery'; that is to say, the work of fantastic imagination may be regarded as a kind of hospital, a place where exhausted people can regain strength and hope.

But, I repeat, Tolkien has, to some extent, undermined his own case: primarily, by sticking to the tradition of 'the little man'. Presumably there is a psychological reason for this: Tolkien feels that the quiet, modest chap, who is capable of heroic exertion under stress, is a more satisfactory hero than Siegfried or Lancelot. There may be some truth in this: but in the way it is worked out in *The Hobbit* and *Lord of the Rings*, it furnishes ammunition for critics who acuse him of sentimentality. In fact, I suspect that Tolkien's choice of the 'little' hero may have been largely a matter of pure chance. Tolkien's work 'snowballed'; it grew by accident. One can see this process clearly in the various books from *The Hobbit* to *Smith of Wootton Major* (1967). *The Hobbit*, like *Alice in Wonderland*, began as a story for children—literally a story told to his own children. Stylistically, it has a casual, careless air. 'In a hole in the ground there lived a hobbit. Not a nasty, dirty, wet hole, filled with the ends of worms and an oozy smell, nor yet a dry, bare, sandy hole with nothing in it to sit down on or to eat; it was a hobbit-hole, and that means comfort., This style is very different from the slightly pretentious style of *Smith of Wootton Major*, which is a little too obviously biblical and poetical.

The story is also distinctly tailored for children. The comforts of the hobbit-hole are listed, and Tolkien enjoys talking about tea and toast and cakes in front of a roaring fire; it is very much a Walt Disney kind of world. When the dwarfs (or dwarves, as Tolkien prefers to call them, for some philological reason) start arriving one by one, until the house is overflowing with them, you can imagine the children squealing with laughter, and saying 'How many more?'

The basic Tolkien formula emerges very quickly. There is a certain realism in the descriptions of difficult journeys, reminiscent of *The Thirty Nine Steps* or *Kidnapped*. He likes describing travels through imaginary landscapes, and he produces the same blend of poetry and adventure and discomfort that one finds in Belloc. He has an excellent imagination for sudden adventures, like the scene with the trolls in the second chapter of *The Hobbit*, where the whole party nearly ends up being eaten by these hairy monsters. The grown up reader finds it exciting because the trolls are sufficiently like gangsters or Nazi thugs to produce the sense that we are talking about something real. Already, Tolkien is showing the ability to write on two levels—for children and adults—that makes *The Lord of the Rings* so successful. One might say that Tolkien had made the important discovery that there is really no need to assume that children and adults have different tastes; what will excite one will excite the other. Also worth noting is that the scene with the trolls is pulled back

from the edge of being too 'scary' for children with the comic climax out of 'The Brave Little Tailor'—the trolls being induced to fight among themselves by imagining that one of their number is playing tricks on the others.

Towards the end, the book begins to lose impetus as a 'fairy story'; the events slow down; the wait on the Lonely Mountain is altogether more 'real' than the earlier scenes. In the conventional fairy story, Bilbo Baggins would kill the dragon by a clever strategem; in *The Hobbit*, the dragon is killed almost arbitrarily 'off stage' by Bard, one of the lake men. The quarrel that then follows—between the dwarves, who have now regained their treasure, and the lake men—is again a realistic touch, indicating that Tolkien is beginning to enjoy the adventure—and battle—for its own sake. Any good literary psychologist might have prophesied that *The Hobbit* would be followed by a more carefully realistic novel. And from the unflagging invention of *The Hobbit*, he might also have guessed that it would be longer.

According to Tolkien, *The Lord of the Rings* was begun shortly after publication of *The Hobbit* (1938-9). He says (in the preface to *Tree and Leaf*), 'At about the time we had reached Bree (i.e. Chapter 9), and I had then no more notion than (the Hobbits) had of what had become of Gandalf or who Strider was.' *The Fellowship of the Ring* appeared in 1954, so its genesis was lengthy. This is apparent in the book itself, which grad-

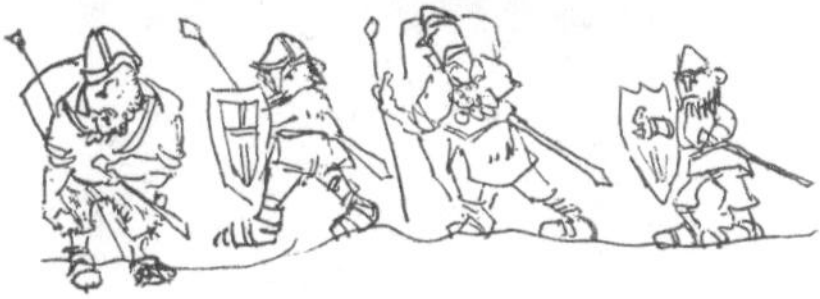

ually changes tone as it goes along. The opening, with the great birthday party, might have been written by Edith Nesbit, or even Enid Blyton; it is still very much in the spirit of a tale told for children, with all the effects children enjoy—descriptions of food and drink, and the rivalries among various relatives. One gets the feeling that Bilbo's sudden disappearance—as he slips on the ring—was not really a calculated part of the story; it is still in the jolly, slapstick spirit of the opening of *The Hobbit.* One can also understand perfectly why it was that Tolkien had no ideas about the development of the plot. His heroes were Setting Off, walking into the unknown, like Belloc or the heroes of Jeffrey Farnol, or Hermann Hesse. The spirit here is very close to Farnol; all the talk about the Brandywine river and the pleasant home comforts of Hobbits are all rather sentimental and 'twee'. Tolkien seems to have invented a kind of secular paradise, a lazy man's heaven, where people have nothing to do but smoke their pipes in the twilight and gossip about the courting couples and next year's May Fair. This paradisial quality is underlined by the information that Hobbits live a great deal longer than human beings—Bilbo is celebrating his eleventy-first birthday. I suspect that it may well be this element, specifically, that jarred on Edmund Wilson, who had harshly criticised T.S. Eliot for escapism. For there can be no doubt that Tolkien himself is emotionally committed to this fairy tale picture of peaceful rural life; it is not intended solely for the children. The 19th century

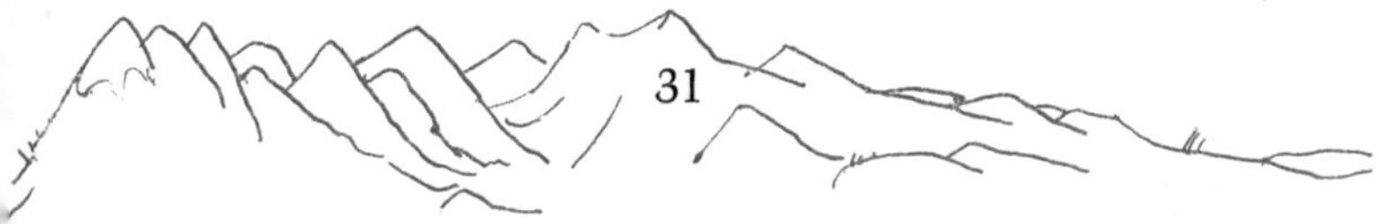

romantics loved painting this kind of a picture—it can be found in Eichendorf, Morike, Gotthelf, Tieck, Jean Paul, and probably derives from Rousseau. The 'realist' objection to it is no longer a matter of 'escapism'. Johnson created a 'happy valley' in *Rasselas*, but the prince finds it boring, and wonders about the nature of the strange urge that makes him want to turn his back on this drowsy peace and seek out conflict and excitement. The evolutionary urge drives man to seek for intenser forms of fulfillment, since his basic urge is for *more* life, more consciousness, and this contentment has an air of stagnation that the healthy mind rejects. (This recognition lies at the centre of my own 'outsider theory': that there are human beings to whom comfort means nothing, but whose happiness consists in following an obscure inner-drive, an 'appetite for reality'.) And yet one might say, in defense of Tolkien, that this evolutionary urge is quite clearly symbolised in the urge that all his characters experience—to seek adventure, to 'go on a journey'. And at the end of *The Return of the King*, Frodo does not 'live happy ever after' in Hobbit land, but has a further journey to make to 'the grey havens'.

Besides, naive or not, this Rousseau-ist nostalgia *is* a part of the charm of the book. The rural comforts of the pub at Bree or Tom Bombadil's house provide the right contrast to the Barrow Downs with their walking dead. It is much the same combination as in the James Bond novels—plenty of the good things of life, with a sharp smell of danger in the air to freshen the appetite.

I imagine that a critic like Wilson would find the first book enjoyable enough, but might begin to grow restive at the Council of Elrond, where one feels that Tolkien is at last beginning to take himself seriously, interposing his own values and writing imitation Norse-saga. He seems to be facing his critics and asking, 'Wasn't their world preferable to ours?' And it is purely a matter of personal feeling. Like Auden, I do not mind sharing the fun, and agreeing for the sake of argument. Another reader may find the style of the speeches unbearably bogus: 'If Gondor, Boromir, has been a stalwart tower, we have played another part. Many evil things there are that your strong walls and bright swords do not stay. You know little of the lands beyond your bounds . . .' and so on. It brings to mind a literary trick perfected by Chesterton, the understatement designed to make your hair tingle, fake simplicity, as in the last sentence of *The Man Who Was Thursday*: 'There he saw the sister of Gregory, the girl with the gold-red hair, cutting lilac before breakfast, with the great unconscious gravity of a girl.' One feels this sentence ought to begin 'And lo!' It led to all the careful heroic understatement of Bulldog Drummond, and the Saint's careless smile as he faces a dozen villainous Chinamen. Robert Graves reacted against it in his historical novels, particularly the Claudius books, making his characters speak in a blunt, colloquial style, to assure the reader that people in ancient Rome were very like people today. So when Tolkien makes his characters talk a language that might

be called Heroicese, some readers feel distinctly 'turned off'. In fact, I found myself skipping these long speeches when I read the book to my children.

All the same, they do not occupy all that much space. The excitement of the book lies in the journey, and in Tolkien's invention. Like the painter Niggle, Tolkien is definitely a creator of scenery. This is all so strongly realised that one feels he ought to collaborate with an illustrator of genius, or perhaps a whole series of illustrators (as in some editions of Shakespeare that have painting by practically every major Victorian artist). If admirers of the book were asked to choose their favourite scenes for illustration, I imagine there would be hundreds, involving forests, rivers, waterfalls, mountains, nearly all of them with some great view into the distance. Wilson objects that none of the characters come alive, and this may be true; but the scenery makes up for it. Tolkien obviously has a very unusual faculty of visualising places: Helm's Deep, Lorien, the White Mountains, the Dead Marshes, the plain of Gorgoroth. Purely as an imaginary travel book, *The Lord of the Rings* is a very remarkable work.

Either you become involved in the fantasy or you don't. If everything in the book 'came off' as Tolkien intends it to, it would certainly be one of the masterpieces of all time. And on a first reading, most of it *does* come off, because the suspense keeps the reader moving so fast that he hardly notices when effects fall flat. On second reading, as he lingers over some of the ex-

cellent descriptions of forests and rivers, he begins to notice that Tom Bombadil is rather a bore (which one might expect of a man who goes around yelling 'Hey dol, merry dol' etc.), that Lothlorien and its elves are a sentimental daydream, that Minas Tirith and its brave fighting men would like an Errol Flynn movie. The core of the book remains Frodo's journey, and this continues to be exciting even after several readings. Edmund Wilson says: 'An impotence of imagination seems to me to sap the whole story. The wars are never dynamic; the ordeals give no sense of strain; the fair ladies would not stir a heartbeat; the horrors would not hurt a fly.' Obviously, a reader's response is very much his own affair; but I cannot help feeling that Tolkien has somehow caught Wilson on the raw in some early page of the book, and that this has induced a mood of bad tempered, carping incredulity that has genuinely made him loathe the whole thing. Where literature is concerned, there *ought* to be some disputing about tastes; it is not enough to say that one man's meat is another man's poison. Some of Wilson's criticisms are valid; Mordor *is* disappointing after the build-up, and one feels that the non-appearance of Sauron is rather an evasion. One might add that Tolkien could have given the story greater depth by working out why the rings exercise such power and how Sauron's kingdom depends upon them. All great art is about the difference between illusion and reality, the everyday world as it appears to us and the reality that lies beneath. The philosopher starts

from the sense that there is a lot of illusion about this world, and that his task is to probe to the reality. It is like a bullfighter's cloak that continually misleads us. Great art somehow produces a sense of glimpses into a deeper order of reality, what lies behind the cloak of the present, and beyond our general narrowness of consciousness. And in spite of all the criticisms, Tolkien's book obviously does this for a very large number of people. So it is hard to see how one can accept Wilson's description of the book as 'long winded volumes of balderdash' as a fair, objective assessment.

But, 'objectively' speaking, *can* one explain the extraordinary appeal of *The Lord of the Rings*? Well, on the simplest level one might regard it as a combination of science fiction and the novel of suspense. Now science fiction is notoriously badly written. It is almost impossible to name a science fiction novel written in the past thirty or forty years (that is, since *Amazing Stories* made the genre so popular) that rises above the clichés of cheap pulp fiction. Even some of the genuine classics of fantasy and suspense, like Merritt's *Seven Footprints to Satan* or the novels of Lovecraft, are so badly written that one must simply accept the atrocious style as a sort of convention. For the average literature—if only moderately sophisticated—reader (say an American college student), Tolkien's style and erudition must make a refreshing change. His world has the charm of innocence, reviving memories of childhood, and the magic of escapism in the non-pejorative sense—the open road,

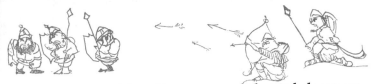

danger and hardship. If one assumes that it belongs on the same shelf as Edgar Rice Burroughs, E.R. Eddison, John Taine, Lovecraft, Van Vogt, then it obviously deserves very high marks indeed. Wilson is simply misleading the reader in evoking Gogol, Poe and Swift, who are aiming at something quite different. (Gogol's early *Dikanka* stories have something in common with Tolkien, and *will* stand comparison; but fantasies like *The Overcoat* and *The Nose* are not remotely related.)

But unlike the writers of science fiction, Tolkien's purpose is not simply to 'astonish'. As we have seen in the essay on fairy stories, he dislikes the modern world, and like Eliot or Yeats, is allowing this negative feeling to trigger a *creative* response. Although it may sound pretentious to say so, *The Lord of the Rings* is a criticism of the modern world and of the values of technological civilisation. It asserts its own values, and tries to persuade the reader that they are preferable to current values. Even the 'poetry', which everybody admits to be no better than average, underlines the feeling of seriousness, that even if the landscapes and adventures bear a superficial resemblance to Edgar Rice Burroughs's Martian novels, the purpose goes deeper. This, I think, defines what my early informants about the book were unable to explain: why it can be taken so seriously. In fact, like *The Waste Land*, it is at once an attack on the modern world and a credo, a manifesto. It stands for a system of values; this is why teenagers write 'Gandalf lives' on the walls of London tubes. Yeats's poems about

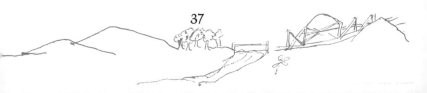

fairyland were intended to be a fist shaken in the face of the modern world. Ruskin once said to Yeats's father that as he walked to the British Museum, he saw the faces of the people grow daily more corrupt; Yeats felt the same. This explains why Auden can take Tolkien so seriously, although his own poetry seems so deliberately 'modern' and anti-escapist.

This comparison raises again the fundamental question. Yeats's fairy poems are very beautiful in their way, but if Yeats had died after he had written them, he would now be merely another minor figure in the 1890s, like Dowson and Johnson. They are valid and important in their way, but Yeats went beyond them. In *Leaf by Niggle*, Tolkien criticises Niggle for ineptitude, for not thinking enough, and it is hard to see any reason why this criticism should not, in the last analysis, be applied to his own work. From an essay on fairy tales to *Smith of Wootton Major* he is stating the same simple proposition: that certain people are dreamers and visionaries, and that although they may seem relatively useless to the community, they embody values that the community cannot afford to forget. This is true enough; but the values embodied in *The Lord of the Rings* are on the same level as those in Yeats's fairy poems. One feels that if he were really pressed to commit himself to a practical solution, he might end in the Catholic church, like Chesterton and Belloc, or at least as a High Anglican, like Eliot. (For all I know, he may be a Catholic or High Anglican; but for the practical purposes of literary criticism, he is a pessimistic Aesthete.) If one is to treat *The Lord of the Rings* as a statement of values, on the same level as the poetry of Eliot or Yeats, or Toynbee's *Study of History*, or the novels of Mann or Hesse, then one must agree that it fails because it is soft in the centre, a romantic anachronism; it should have been published in the 1850s, not the 1950s. Judged by the standards of George MacDonald's *Phantastes*, or *Alice in Wonderland*, or *The Wind in the Willows*, it is a splendid piece of work that will maintain a permanent place. Judged by the standards of a real work of genius and originality, like Daved Lindsay's *Voyage to Arcturus*, it lacks that final cutting edge of moral perception and seriousness. It is a fine book, but it does not belong in the first rank.

Tolkien, I suspect, would not mind this judgment in the least. He obviously enjoyed writing it; millions have enjoyed reading it; that, he would say, is enough. You can't expect him to be a Tolstoy or Dostoevsky as well. His position seems to be that the business of the artist —of *his* type of artist—is to create a kind of tree, as green and alive as possible. The tree will serve its purpose in a world that becomes increasingly urbanised.

Within his own terms, he is obviously right. Whether you accept these terms depends upon whether, like Edmund Wilson, you feel the artist has a 'duty' to the community, to history, to literature, or whatever. My own view of art tends to be less rigorous; I am inclined to feel that there is no point in looking a gift horse in the

mouth. No doubt *The Lord of the Rings* is less significant than it looks at first sight. Perhaps it could have been made more significant if Tolkien had seriously thought-out the ideas he expressed in *Leaf by Niggle*. But perhaps if he had brooded too much on the artist's relation to society, the book wouldn't have got written at all; and then everybody would be worse off.

Note on Tolkien

When I wrote this small book, Tolkien was still alive. It was written originally at the request of a British publisher—of limited editions—who said he wanted to do a book of essays on writers of fantasy; I agreed to do the piece on Tolkien, largely because I had just finished reading The Hobbit and Lord of the Rings to my children for the second or third time. The publisher then decided to issue it as a separate book—perhaps because the other contributors were less prompt than I was.

I have never met Tolkien, and never had any contact with him, except through a brief correspondence in the early sixties. I now regret it; Donald Swann, who set a number of the poems to music, told me he was an amiable and approachable man, and that I ought to call and see him when I was in Oxford. When I had written this essay, I dropped him a line to say that I

41

intended publishing a short book on him, and suggesting that we might meet. In fact, a Dutch 'occult' magazine had suggested I interview him. Alas, the attempt at contact ended as a comedy of non-communication. I received a letter back from Tolkien's solicitor, saying that he was alarmed to hear I had written a book called Tree By Tolkien. That sounded, he said, as if it was written by Tolkien, and therefore conveyed a false impression. In any case, he said, Tolkien was an old man, not in the best of health, and highly sensitive to critical comments about his work. So would I please agree to suppress the work—at least, for the duration of Tolkien's lifetime . . .? The general tone was haughty, as befits one who has been appointed the mouthpiece of a great writer.

I replied that unfortunately it was too late to withdraw the book; it was already at the printers. However, if he was worried about harsh critical comment, he had no cause for concern. It was, on the whole, thoroughly pro-Tolkien. As to the objection that bookshop-browsers might think it a new work by Tolkien, this was unlikely because (a) it was a limited edition that would only be sold to subscribers, and (b) my name would be displayed prominently on the cover. I explained that the title was an oblique reference to Tolkien's own story Leaf by Niggle . . . I ended by saying that it would be kind if he could pass my letter on to Tolkien, or at least to someone in his immediate family, just in case he might be willing to see me.

Evidently the man did not like to be crossed. A short and harsh letter said it was highly unreasonable of me to persist in publishing a book against Tolkein's wishes, and that he still felt the title conveyed a false impression. He ended irritably: 'I have mentioned it to Mr. Tolkien. He does not want to see you.'

I was sorry; not because I couldn't get to see the old man—after all, he was ill and more than eighty years old, and no doubt I shall be just as unwilling to see strangers at that age—but because it seemed a pity that a kindly and courteous man should be represented by anyone so rude. I did receive an apologetic letter from a girl at his publishers, saying that for some time he had been too ill to see anyone, and that his family were concerned in case he was upset by attacks on himself— from which I gather that some of the patronizing comments of critics had caused offense. I replied that it was a pity I hadn't been able to interview him—think how posterity would have welcomed an interview of Shakespeare by John Milton. I hoped the comment might tease her into sending the letter to Tolkien, but it didn't. A couple of weeks later, copies of the book arrived, and I sent one care of his publishers. The day after I sent it, I heard news of his death. I also sent two copies of the book to W. H. Auden, who had told me he would be seeing Tolkien in Oxford, asking him, if he got the chance, to smuggle one in to Tolkien. A few days after that, I heard on the radio that Auden had died. . . .

Re-reading the book a year later, I find that I have

nothing to add to it. But it strikes me that Tolkien's popularity was essentially a part of the 'occult revival' of the 1960s. Of course, he deserved it; his fantasy is a classic, and will undoubtedly live as long as Alice in Wonderland and Gulliver's Travels, and probably longer than the fantasies of George MacDonald and C. S. Lewis, being easier to read. But that is no guarantee that a book achieves the fame it deserves; Mervyn Peake's Gormenghast trilogy reached a wide audience only after his death; and David Lindsay's Voyage to Arcturus—fundamentally a greater book than The Lord of the Rings because it has more to say—is still virtually unknown, at least in England.

The reason for Tolkien's enormous popularity in the sixties was not simply that he is a fine storyteller, and one of the greatest exponents of the art of 'escapism' in the history of literature, but because his ideas suddenly struck an answering chord in young readers—I apologize for the cliché. In 2001—A Space Odyssey, Arthur C. Clarke had popularised the notion that perhaps men were not the earliest intelligent life on earth; perhaps there had been visitors from other planets who had deliberately 'helped' us. Erich von Däniken's Chariots of the Gods? (serialised in a Sunday newspaper under the title: Was God a Spaceman?) made the same suggestion in more detail, and in spite of its slapdash presentation and a tendency to harangue the reader, it became a world best-seller. At the same time, H. P. Lovecraft's stories, with their legend of 'ancient old ones' who inhabited the earth long before human beings, and who destroyed themselves through the practice of black magic, suddenly found a wider audience than he had ever known in his lifetime—or indeed, for many decades after his death. I had discovered Tolkien and Lovecraft at about the same time, in 1960, and had written of both of them in The Strength to Dream, pointing out the similarities. 'Far, far below the deepest delvings of the Dwarves, the world is gnawed by nameless things. Even Sauron knows them not. They are older than he . . .' This could easily be Lovecraft. The appendices to The Lord of the Rings also carry the history of Middle Earth back to these far ages before men and hobbits. (Oddly enough, though, Tom Bombadil was supposed to be alive then—a point that emphasizes that Tolkien's imagination is much more cheerful than Lovecraft's.) Tolkien has this desire to create a whole world, and supply it with remote origins. He is expressing a human craving to reach beyond the everyday boundaries of human existence. And this, I think, is perhaps his real significance. Brian Aldiss has a science fiction story called Outside that captures something essential about human existence. Six people are living in a windowless house; every day food appears, but no one asks where it comes from, or what they are doing there. Eventually, it turns out that five of the six are aliens from space, who can imitate the form of human beings. They have been captured and placed in the room to force them to reveal their identity. Only one is

45

a true human being, and because he is passive and seems incurious about his situation, the aliens are also passive, thereby, the author implies, revealing that they are not human. For human beings get curious, want to know what they are doing here. . . .

That is not quite true. The great majority of western literature, from Homer to Jane Austen and Trollope, takes the world in which we find ourselves for granted, and asks no awkward questions. For more than two centuries now, science has declared that such questions would be pointless, for we are simply objects, like other objects, in a material universe. The modern philosophy known as logical positivism also asserts that 'metaphysical' questions are meaningless. We are here, and that's that. . . . But periodically, human beings seem to experience a compulsion to know *why* they are here—or at least, to ask the question. It began to happen midway through the last century, with writers like Kierkegaard, Tolstoy, Dostoevsky. And the same curiosity took the form of an 'occult revival' in the last three decades of the 19th century. By 1918, that was all over, and Wittgenstein had already written the Tractatus Logico-Philosophicus, with its insistence that it is meaningless to ask questions about a 'beyond', because there is no beyond; it is a linguistic misunderstanding. Wittgenstein was by no means happy about his own conclusion, as his tortured life—reminiscent in many ways of Tolstoy's—reveals; but logical positivists like A. J. Ayer were delighted to use his arguments to support their

46

view that life is exactly what it seems, no more and no less.

In the 1950s and early sixties, when the positivists and 'linguistic analysts' dominated the philosophy departments of almost every major university in the world, I would never have believed that the day would come when they would be not only discredited, but half-forgotten. Now it has come, I'm not sure it's entirely a good thing—there is something of the positivist in my make-up, as may be inferred from this essay. But the change has certainly come. The new generation is interested in Tolkien, Gurdjieff, Hesse, John Cowper Powys, and in wide, far-ranging speculations about the universe and the distant past. Whether this interest will exhaust itself—as it did at the turn of the present century—depends largely on the 'spearhead', on scientists and psychologists and parapsychologists who are trying to widen the boundaries of our knowledge. Obviously, Tolkien does not belong among these. But he belongs among the great stimulators of the 'occult revival'—in fact, he is perhaps even its originator. For a man who only set out to write an 'escapist' fairy story, this is a remarkable achievement.

This chapbook series, edited by
Robert Durand (Yes! Press) and Noel Young
(Capra Press), is printed in Santa Barbara
by Capra Press. This edition was especially
designed by Graham and Caitlin Mackintosh.
This is the twentieth title in the series,
published May 1974. Two hundred numbered copies,
signed by the author, were handbound.